For Tamsin and Mike Abbott, who love the woods and
all things wild – and for all the bears of the world
J.M.

JANETTA OTTER-BARRY BOOKS

Text and Illustrations copyright © Jackie Morris 2014

The right of Jackie Morris to be identified as the author and illustrator
of this Work has been asserted by her in accordance
with the Copyright, Designs and Patent Act, 1988.

First published in Great Britain by Frances Lincoln Children's Books,
74-77 White Lion Street, London N1 9PF
www.franceslincoln.com

This edition first published in Great Britain and the USA in 2014

Cataloguing in Publication Data for this book is available from the British Library.

ISBN: 978-1-84780-516-4

Printed in China

9 8 7 6 5 4 3 2 1

www.jackiemorris.co.uk

Something about a Bear

Jackie Morris

Let me tell you something –
something about a bear.

Where the water churns with salmon,
thick and rich with leaping fishes,
there the Brown Bear stands and catches the
wild king of the river. On the shore the young
bears watch him; still others swim the waters,
but they are careful not to challenge, for
he is strongest of them all.

In the wildest lands of China, in the forests and the mountains, lives the white-and-black Giant Panda, hidden from the world.

Born as soft and small as peaches, Panda's child grows fast on bear milk, while his mother eats the bamboo that grows green on mountain slopes.

Through the forest, hunting termites and the honey hives of bees, where the mangos and the fruit trees grow in plenty, walks the shaggy-coated Sloth Bear.

With her cubs aboard her strong back she keeps them safe from danger, for there are tigers in the forests, and wild dogs and leopards too.

Up in the crowns of tall trees, in the softest nests of green leaves, the Spectacled Bear sunbathes through the heat of the day. As she nurses cubs she sings to them, safe high up in the treetops, between cloud forest and jungle, where fruit grows the richest.

By dawn light and dusk light the great Moon Bear of Asia hunts and searches, for insects, and for honey, nuts and berries. Shining out from her black fur the crescent moon glows brightly, a gift given by the gods to the creature of the forest. Where the forest meets the snowline she watches from her bear's nest for the wild leopard of the mountains, who hunts the higher ground.

Swimming through the water, where the ice-flow meets the ocean, lives the great white Polar Bear. Hunting seals on silent paws, hushed as gentle falling snow. Skin black, hollow fur, warm bear in a world of ice.

Fiercer than a leopard, fearless, strong and wild, the Sun Bear sleeps in treetops through the burning heat of day. In the cool of night he searches for the sweet nests of honey, ripping trees apart for insects. Smallest of all bears, coat as short as velvet, huge claws, great teeth, even tigers fear him.

Beside the lakes and in the forests Black Bear fishes in the water, growing fat upon the salmon and on berries from the bushes. In the coldest part of winter Black Bear curls and sleeps till springtime, in a darkened den or hollow of a fallen tree. Fur in many different colours, black and cinnamon and honey, white Black Bears are rarest, sacred spirits of the forest.

So, let me tell you something,
something about a bear.

Of all the bears in the wide wild world,
the very best bear of all is...

your bear.

Brown Bear

Brown Bears are the most widely distributed species of bear in the world, found in parts of eastern Europe, Russia, India, China, Canada and the USA. Once they ranged right across Asia, Europe and America, even in Britain until they were hunted to extinction there, around AD 1000. Of all the Brown Bears the Kodiak Bear is the largest, as big as a Polar Bear. They grow to this size because of the feasts of salmon that they enjoy each year. Brown Bears have huge territories, large teeth, big claws and they can run at 50 miles an hour. Brown Bears hibernate in winter. When a bear hibernates its body temperature drops by two degrees. Its heart rate can drop from 40-70 beats a minute to only 10 beats a minute.

Giant Panda

Pandas are mostly herbivores, eating bamboo, though now and again they eat meat. Their heads are large and they have big, strong jaw muscles for chewing and crunching bamboo. Like most bears the Giant Panda is a solitary animal, preferring to live alone. Pandas do not hibernate in winter. The nourishment they gain from eating bamboo is never enough to build up the layers of fat they would need to hibernate. Pandas live in the remote mountains and forests of China. There are thought to be fewer than 1,600 Giant Pandas in the wild. A newborn Panda is about the same size as a block of butter. In a lifetime a mother Panda will give birth to only five or six cubs. The cubs stay with their mother for up to three years.

Sloth Bear

Sloth Bears love to feed on termites. They use their strong paws and huge claws to rip open the tough nests of termites. Then they push their noses in tight, and blow and suck the termites and eggs through a gap in their front teeth. Very noisy eaters, you can sometimes hear them feeding from far away. They also love to eat fruit (mangos and figs), as well as flowers. Sloth Bears have long shaggy coats, and they live in the forests of Southern Asia. Sloth Bear cubs ride on their mothers' backs as they move around the forest. This gives the cubs protection from the leopards, tigers and wild dogs that share their territories with the bears.

Spectacled Bear

The Spectacled Bear is South America's only bear. They can be found from Panama to Venezuela. Their favourite habitat is the cloud forests, as high as 4,300 metres (14,000 feet) above sea level. Their name is derived from their facial markings, and unlike other bears they have a short snout. The Spectacled Bear sleeps in nests in the trees during the day. They eat mostly fruit and nuts, but also rabbits, birds and cacti, berries, grasses and tubors. It is thought that there are only 3,000 Spectacled Bears left in the wild. The bears are threatened by loss of habitat due to logging, and also they are hunted for their fur, paws and bear bile. The Spectacled Bear is the last remaining short-faced bear. Once it had a larger relative, The Florida Spectacled Bear, larger than a Polar Bear.

Find out more about bears at these conservation websites:
http://www.hauserbears.com/
http://www.polarbearsinternational.org/
http://www.moonbears.org/
http://bearwithus.org/
http://www.bsbcc.org.my/
http://www.worldlandtrust.org/

Moon Bear or Asiatic Black Bear

These bears have many names: Moon Bear, Asiatic Black Bear, Himalayan Black Bear, Tibetan Black Bear. Moon Bears are wonderful climbers and love nuts and honey. They roam over huge areas searching for food. Moon Bears live in forests, hills and mountains. Where Moon Bears are found in northern regions they will hibernate, building up layers of fat during the summer, eating nuts and berries, to see them through their period of sleep. Moon Bears are endangered by deforestation, and also by the trade in bear parts for Chinese medicine, including bear bile. Some bears are kept in cages where bile can be extracted from them. Moon Bears are also kept as 'dancing bears' by street musicians, who earn their money playing music while the bears dance.

Polar Bears

Polar Bears are the largest of all the bears. They have an amazing sense of smell, and can sniff out a seal pup through a metre (three feet) of ice. Polar Bears have black skin. Their hair is not white, but transparent, and works as a conductor of heat to their bodies. They move slowly, as despite their freezing environment their black skin and unique hair mean that they overheat easily. To cool off they sometimes lie on their backs with their paws in the air, as they are able to lose heat through the soles of their feet. Polar Bears are wonderful swimmers. They use their huge paws, the size of dinner plates, to paddle through water at speeds of up to six miles an hour. Their back legs work as rudders. They have been found swimming up to 100 miles from land. Polar Bears eat seal and walrus, but can also eat beluga whales and narwhals. They have a unique digestion, because they seldom drink, so usually feast on the fat of the animal and leave the meat for scavengers. While females make dens, scraped out from ice on south-facing slopes, the males are nomadic, roaming for hundreds of miles. The females give birth to tiny cubs between November and January, and the cubs grow in the den, emerging into their white, cold world in March and April.

Sun Bear

Smallest of all the bears, the Sun Bear is about the same size as a large dog. It gets its name from the golden crescent it wears on its chest. Sun Bears live in the forests of Asia. With long claws and bowed legs, they are as happy climbing trees as on the ground. Sun Bears are fierce. Despite their small size their teeth are as long as the teeth of a tiger. Sun Bears sleep through the heat of the day, high up in treetops. The translation of their name in Malaysian, *basindo nan tenggil*, is "he who likes to sit high". Sun Bears have really long tongues which they use for licking termites from logs and honey from bee hives. The Sun Bears' skin looks as if it is too big for them. Their expressive faces often have wrinkles and frowns. If grabbed by a predator, they can turn and twist inside their loose-fitting skin, to attack with sharp claws.

American Black Bear

American Black Bears come in many different colours, black, cinnamon, honey, blue and even white. The bears can be found from the Pacific to the Atlantic coasts, from Canada to Mexico. White Black Bears are also known as Spirit Bears or Kermode bears. Black Bears are the smallest of the three bear species found in northern America. They are also thought to be the cleverest. There are about 600,000 Black Bears in northern America. Most Black Bears will hibernate in dens found in hollowed trees or forest caves. When bears hibernate they feed on the body fat they have build up over the summer when food is plentiful. Black Bears are omnivorous. They eat nuts and berries, fruit and insects, honey, deer, fish, grasses, sandwiches from campers when they can find them, and carrion.

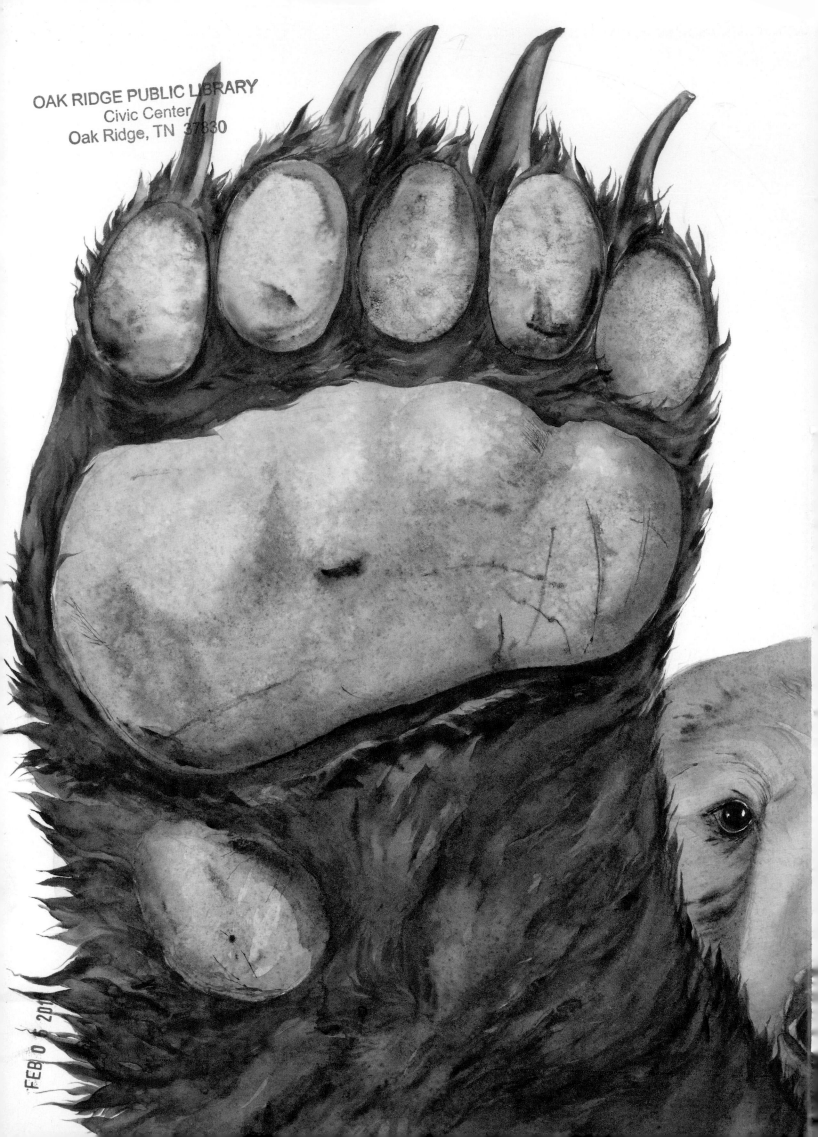